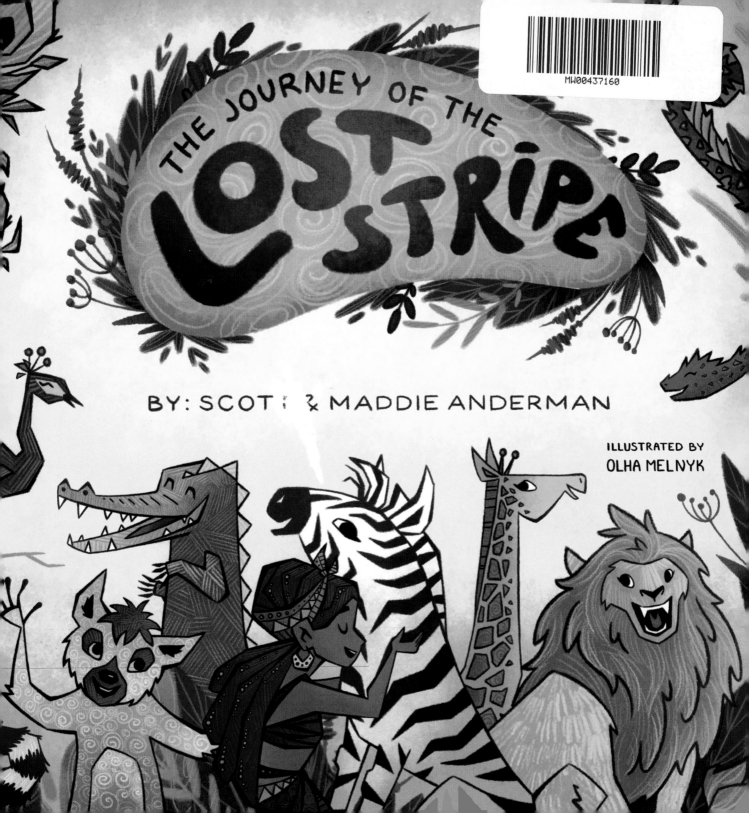

THE JOURNEY OF THE LOST STRIPE

BY: SCOTT & MADDIE ANDERMAN

ILLUSTRATED BY
OLHA MELNYK

"The Journey of the Lost Stripe" is a work of fiction. Names, characters, places and incidents are the products of the author's imagination, or are used fictitiously. Any resemblance to actual events, locales, characters or persons, living or dead, is entirely coincidental.

Library of congress control number: 2021919752
ISBN : 978-1-68489-257-0

First Paperback Edition 2021. Kindle Edition.
Phoenix, Arizona, United States of America.

Illustrations by Olha Melnyk

Travel through the African savannah with the tale of a unique zebra named Lulu. On the journey to find her lost stripe, she gains the lessons of true friendship, the gift of giving, and the joy of self-acceptance.

Lulu awakes from an afternoon nap and something is missing. One of her zebra stripes is gone! The little zebra embarks on a journey through the colorful savannah in search of her lost stripe.

With the help of her human and animal friends, Lulu finds so much more than a stripe. On each page, Lulu gains the life lessons of giving, friendship and self-love. In "The Journey of the Lost Stripe", Lulu learns that differences can be beautiful, and confidence comes from being exactly who you are today.

LOVE YOURSELF...
No matter what.

This story is dedicated to
my **amazing daughter**,
Madeline Ciel Anderman.

What if your "stripe" was your ability to walk? What if one day, it disappeared. Maddie was born with a rare muscular condition which made it progressively more difficult to walk. Among many things, friendships have helped us realize the truly special things in life. We feel blessed to have our family and friends beside us always.

Our journey is full of adventures.

May we all continue practicing to love ourselves unconditionally along the way. Madeline, not a day goes by that I do not feel you are the most beautiful and unique character I will ever have the chance to meet.

It is a **great honor**
to be your father.

I love you.

May your life's "necklace"
be extraordinary!

Portion of proceeds to benefit the RYRI foundation.
For more information, visit https://www.ryr1.org

Glossary

(These terms are used in the book)

Africa	:	Earth's second largest continent, with many really cool and unique animals.
Savannah	:	A grassy ecosystem in Africa, where trees are widely scattered, but feed and protect animals from the sun.
Lake Tanganyika	:	An African 'Great Lake' in Southeast Africa, and the longest freshwater lake in the world.
Acacia Tree	:	The Giraffe's favorite tree which resembles an umbrella.
Baobab Tree	:	A very tall "Tree of life" found in Madagascar. Can live over 1,000 years.
Zebra	:	A striped horse that roams in a dazzle throughout Africa. A foal is a young zebra or horse.
Dazzle	:	A group of zebras.
Peacock	:	A large bird with colorful feathers that lives in Africa and Asia. They can't fly very far.
Ring-tailed Lemur	:	A large primate only found in Madagascar with black and white rings on its tail.
Bush Viper	:	A venomous and sometimes colorful snake that slithers through Africa.
Giraffe	:	The tallest living land mammal with long legs and an even longer neck. Its body has patterns for camouflage.
Lion	:	A very large and feared cat that lives in Africa. Sometimes referred to as the "King of the Jungle".
Mane	:	The hair around a male lion's neck that makes him easy to spot.
Reptile	:	A cold-blooded animal that typically has a special type of skin made of bone or scales.
Swahili	:	The common language of Southeast African people and Tanzania.
Jambo	:	A friendly "Hello" in Swahili.
Mamba	:	Means "Crocodile" in Swahili.
Tausi	:	Means "Peacock" in Swahili.
Nyoka	:	Means "Snake" in Swahili.
Twiga	:	Means "Giraffe" in Swahili.
Nzuri	:	Means "Beautiful" in Swahili.
Karibu	:	Means "You're welcome" in Swahili.

Baobab
Tree

Readers and listeners together are encouraged to play along and **make up the sound** or **act out** the words between these [colored brackets]

One beautiful afternoon, a **friendly** zebra named **Lulu** awoke from a nap in the African savannah.

"[Yaaawwwhhum]" yawned Lulu. She was feeling warm and decided to splash around in Lake Tanganyika.

She loved the feeling of the cool water under the **hot** sun.

While splashing around in the water, Lulu noticed her reflection. Something was strangely different this time. She was **MISSING A STRIPE!**

"Oh, No!

Where did my stripe go?" she thought. "I feel so strange without it. What will my friends think if I am not able to blend in with them? What will they say if I am different now?"

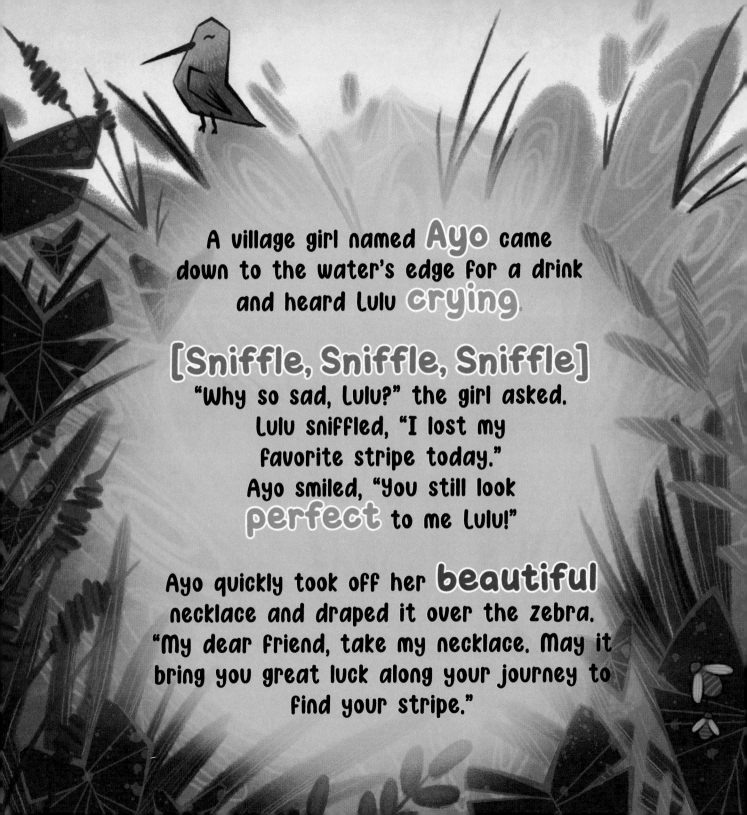

A village girl named Ayo came
down to the water's edge for a drink
and heard Lulu crying.

[Sniffle, Sniffle, Sniffle]
"Why so sad, Lulu?" the girl asked.
Lulu sniffled, "I lost my
favorite stripe today."
Ayo smiled, "You still look
perfect to me Lulu!"

Ayo quickly took off her beautiful
necklace and draped it over the zebra.
"My dear friend, take my necklace. May it
bring you great luck along your journey to
find your stripe."

Lulu was comforted
by her **kindness** and **softly** whispered,
"Thank you, Ayo." Ayo whispered back "Karibu, Lulu."

Up from underneath the water rose
a **big**, **green**, **hungry** alligator.

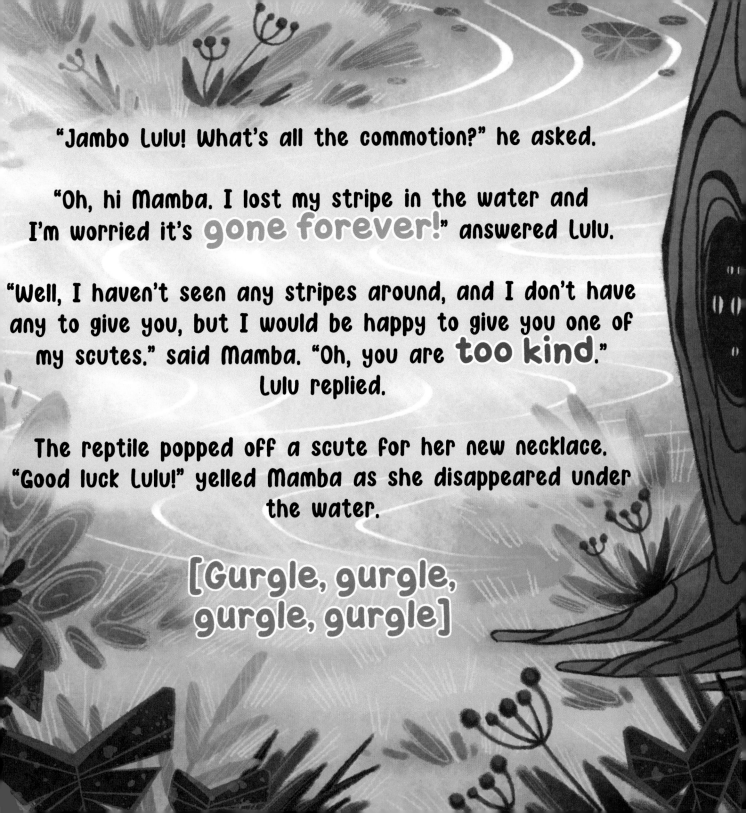

"Jambo Lulu! What's all the commotion?" he asked.

"Oh, hi Mamba. I lost my stripe in the water and I'm worried it's gone forever!" answered Lulu.

"Well, I haven't seen any stripes around, and I don't have any to give you, but I would be happy to give you one of my scutes." said Mamba. "Oh, you are too kind." Lulu replied.

The reptile popped off a scute for her new necklace. "Good luck Lulu!" yelled Mamba as she disappeared under the water.

[Gurgle, gurgle, gurgle, gurgle]

Lulu left the lake sad and afraid of what was ahead, when she came across a **peacock** on the grassy shores. "Hi Tausi, any chance you have seen a zebra stripe around?" asked Lulu. "I have lost one today."

"No, [wak wak]." squawked Tausi. "I am so sorry. I would be more than happy to give you one of my eyespots [wak wak], if it made you feel better."

Tausi plucked a **shiny feather** and offered it to Lulu. "It's so delicate and precious, won't you need it?" asked Lulu.

"You have always been so **nice** to me Lulu, and plus it looks better on you anyway [wak wak]."
The peacock winked.
Lulu then stuck the **exotic** feather in her new necklace and continued on.

Just then...
something slithered underneath Lulu.
"[EEEwwoowwaa!!]
What is that!" she screamed.

"Oh, it's just you Nyoka. You scared me!"
"Sssuper to sssee you Lulu, isss that a new
necklasss?" hissed Nyoka.

"It is. My friends gave it to me because I lost
something really important to me. Nyoka... can I
ask you something? Do you think I look funny
without my middle stripe?" Lulu wondered.

"No, I like your new sssence of ssstyle, Lulu.
May I offer you one of my scalesss to add to
your new look?" asked Nyoka, instantly sliding
a glimmering scale over to Lulu.

"I would love such a **pretty** scale, thank you!" said Lulu adding the vibrant scale to her fancy new necklace.

"Cccertainly welcome, be sssafe!" said the **colorful** bush viper as she went on her slithering way.

After some time,
Lulu **rested** in the shade of a
nearby Baobab tree. "Where could that
stripe have gone?" thought Lulu.

Just then a fruit
squashed beside her from up above.

[Sssppllaaattt]
Lulu looked up to find a smiling lemur.
"Jambo Lulu! How you be?"

"Hi, Lemmie. I am feeling really down today
because I've **lost** my stripe." sighed Lulu.

"**Silly** zebra, don't you know life is about
more than just **stripes?** Here though,
have one of my rings if it makes you feel better."

"No, I couldn't take one of your rings, I just couldn't."
said Lulu, but Lemmie was already climbing off
with his juicy fruit.

Lulu was still upset about losing her stripe, but
was also happy that all of her friends cared
so much to make her feel better.

She was admiring her pretty necklace
when she came to a giraffe eating his
favorite leaves from an Acacia tree.

It was Twiga. "How goes it, Lu?" said Twiga
as he reached for a tasty snack.
"[Whatrr ronderfool day taday.]"
he said while munching on a mouthful
of veggies.

"I don't know." Lulu frowned.
"It started off really bad, but it's looking
better now. I have this pretty necklace my
friends gave me." Lulu glowed.

"That is dazzling! You must have
really nice friends." said Twiga.

"I lost one of my stripes today and I have been sad ever since. I worry that I won't fit in anymore. I **worry** that the dazzle won't **accept** me for who I am." Lulu began to cry thinking about it.

"Well little buddy, if you look closely out there, everyone in the herd is **different**. Each of us is **unique** in our own way. That's why it all works. Maybe one of my patterns would help cheer you up, I've got plenty." said Twiga handing Lulu her very own giraffe spot.

"Really, you too would do that for me?" Lulu gleamed as she showed off her new pattern. Twiga admired her as he headed off for another tasty Acacia tree, "Nzuri! Nzuri! You are **beautiful**, my friend!"

Lulu was deep in thought about her situation. She was not sure how to feel about her missing stripe anymore. She soon realized she had **accidentally** entered the territory of the **king**.

"**[ROOOOOOAAAAAAAAARRRR!!!]**"
shouted a big lion, it was the
feared King Mkuu.

"Why is it that you enter here, little
zebra?" **growled** the king. Lulu
trembled. "Oh no, please do not **eat** me!
I am only looking for my lost stripe."

"You certainly are an interesting looking
zebra, aren't you? Why do you look
so **delightful?**" asked the lion.
"Well, I guess you are right...
I do look kinda nice." said Lulu
blushing a little.

"My friends have given me all of these nice
gifts to cheer me up on my journey."

"Friends?" frowned King Mkuu. "I do not have any friends. How do you get them to stay?" he asked.

Lulu paused for a second, "Well, by giving, I guess... you can give friends your time, your attention, kind words, thoughtful gifts, and when they are sad, make sure to always tell them **how important** they are to you."

The lion shyly asked, "Hmmmm... Lulu, may I **give** you something and call you my friend?" Lulu smiled, "I would be **honored** ".

"Well then, here is a **fluff** of my mane for my new friend." said the lion.

"A king's **mane!** WOW!! It is so soft. Can I come back and see you again, King Mkuu?" asked Lulu. "You are **always** welcome on my land. Thank you for being my first friend ever and good luck on your quest." purred Mkuu.

Lulu's journey had brought her back home and she saw her dazzle of zebras off in the distance. She was still feeling a little **embarrassed** about her missing stripe, but she also felt something more. Something really, really good!

Her caring friends had given her the **courage** and the **confidence** to finally show the other zebras what made her different. Her true self.

As she trotted close,
she came across a younger zebra
crying in the high grass.
"What is wrong little foal?" Lulu asked.

"I woke up **without** one of my stripes today
and I don't know what to do." sniffled the young
zebra. Lulu was amazed. "You may not believe
this, but me too! I was so sad at first, but then I
realized there is more to us than just our stripes."
said Lulu. "Here, **take one of mine!**" Lulu
proudly said as she placed one of her stripes on
her new found friend.

"**[Sniffle sniffle]**
Thank you!" said the little zebra.

Lulu was missing two stripes now, but she was the absolute **happiest** zebra in the whole savannah, and definitely the most **unique!**

Lulu **shined** because she realized she already had everything she needed. She understood now that life is fuller when you learn to **appreciate** those who love you, and to love yourself, **no matter what!**

What do they mean?

- Beautiful
- Commotion
- Comforted
- Confidence
- Courage
- Dazzling
- Delicate
- Embarrassed
- Exotic
- Frowned
- Gift
- Important

- Kindness
- Precious
- Quest
- Reflection
- Squished
- Strange
- Sunset
- Thoughtful
- Unique
- Vibrant
- Winked
- Yawned

Can you find these words in the story?

Continue the Conversation

- Have you ever lost something really important to you?
- Do you know anyone who lost a "stripe"?
- How do we make friends?
- How do we keep friendships?
- Why did Lulu's friends give Lulu gifts?
- What could we do for a friend that is sad?
- Who was your favorite character in the book?
- Why was Lulu happy in the end, even though she was missing two stripes?
- Do you agree with Lulu about what makes life great?
- Can you remember how many animal characters were in the book?
- Can you remember the animals names?
- Can you remember what each animal gave to Lulu?
- Can you remember some of the African words and their meanings?
- Can you count every animal in this book (even the hidden ones)?
- Do you know where Africa is? Can you name other African animals?

May your life's 'necklace'
be extraordinary!

Made in the USA
Middletown, DE
15 December 2021

55982011R00022